Owlet's First Flight

MITRA MODARRESSI

G. P. Putnam's Sons

An Imprint of Penguin Group (USA) Inc.

Little Owlet wakes on a moonlit night.
His mama says, "It's time you took flight."

"Your brothers and sisters have all flown the nest.
I'm sure you can be as brave as the rest."

"But it's dark," he cries.
"I might lose my way."

"Owls see fine in the dark!" she says.
"That's when they play."

A dip, a drop, but now he is steady.

Fly, little Owlet,
tonight you are ready!

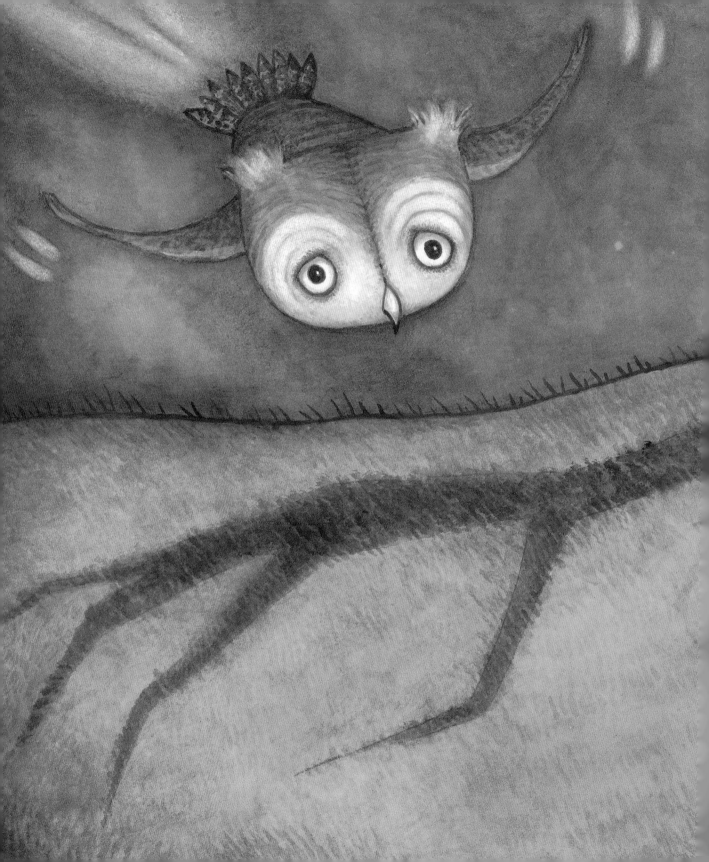

Eek! A dark shadow! What can it be?

Oh, just some branches
of an old tree.

And now little Owlet
hears a loud *pop!*

But it's only some acorns
that happened to drop.

And *what* is that horrible
bang-clanging sound?

Just some other night critters messing around.

Look at you, little Owlet,
out on your own!
The places you've seen,
the miles you've flown.

Oh, what an evening! An owlet's first flight!

But it's time to head home now—
the sky's almost light.

He soars through the woods, back to his tree.
He's the last one in. Mama's proud as can be.

Now little Owlet is ready to rest.
Safe with his family, snug in his nest.

With thanks to the Department of Ornithology and Mammalogy,
California Academy of Sciences.

G. P. PUTNAM'S SONS · A division of Penguin Young Readers Group.
Published by The Penguin Group.
Penguin Group (USA) Inc., 375 Hudson Street, New York, NY 10014, U.S.A.
Penguin Group (Canada), 90 Eglinton Avenue East, Suite 700, Toronto, Ontario M4P 2Y3, Canada (a division of Pearson Penguin Canada Inc.).
Penguin Books Ltd, 80 Strand, London WC2R 0RL, England.
Penguin Ireland, 25 St. Stephen's Green, Dublin 2, Ireland (a division of Penguin Books Ltd.).
Penguin Group (Australia), 250 Camberwell Road, Camberwell, Victoria 3124, Australia (a division of Pearson Australia Group Pty Ltd).
Penguin Books India Pvt Ltd, 11 Community Centre, Panchsheel Park, New Delhi - 110 017, India.
Penguin Group (NZ), 67 Apollo Drive, Rosedale, Auckland 0632, New Zealand (a division of Pearson New Zealand Ltd).
Penguin Books (South Africa) (Pty) Ltd, 24 Sturdee Avenue, Rosebank, Johannesburg 2196, South Africa.
Penguin Books Ltd, Registered Offices: 80 Strand, London WC2R 0RL, England.

Design by Marikka Tamura. Text set in Sinclair Medium Script.
The art was done in watercolors on Fabriano hot press paper.
Library of Congress Cataloging-in-Publication Data is available upon request.
Modarressi, Mitra. Owlet's first flight / Mitra Modarressi. p. cm.
Summary: A hesitant young owl leaves his nest for the first time and explores the nighttime on his own.
[1. Stories in rhyme. 2. Owls—Fiction. 3. Flight—Fiction. 4. Fear of the dark—Fiction.] I. Title.
PZ8.3.M712 Ow 2012 [E]—dc23 2011013306
ISBN 978-0-399-25526-7
1 3 5 7 9 10 8 6 4 2